# When the River Ran Backward

# When the River Ran Backward

Emily Crofford

Carolrhoda Books, Inc./Minneapolis

# Adventures in Time Books

*This book is available in two editions:*
Hardcover by Carolrhoda Books, Inc.
Softcover by First Avenue Editions
Divisions of Lerner Publishing Group
241 First Avenue North
Minneapolis, MN 55401 U.S.A.

Website address: www.lernerbooks.com

Library of Congress Cataloging-in-Publication Data

Crofford, Emily.
    When the River Ran Backward / by Emily Crofford.
        p.   cm. — (Adventures in time books)
    Summary: In the process of coping with a series of earthquakes which strike the frontier town of New Madrid in 1811 and 1812, fifteen-year-old Laurel discovers an unexpected romance.
    ISBN 1-57505-305-5 (hardcover)—ISBN 1-57505-488-4 (pbk.)
    1. Earthquakes—Missouri—New Madrid—Juvenile fiction.
    [1. Earthquakes—Missouri—New Madrid—Fiction.] 2. New Madrid (Mo.)—Fiction.] I. Title. II. Series.
    PZ7.C873 Wh  2000
    [Fic]—dc21                                              99-050527

Manufactured in the United States of America
1 2 3 4 5 6 - BP - 05 04 03 02 01 00

*In loving memory of William T. Cooper*
*of New Madrid and Memphis*

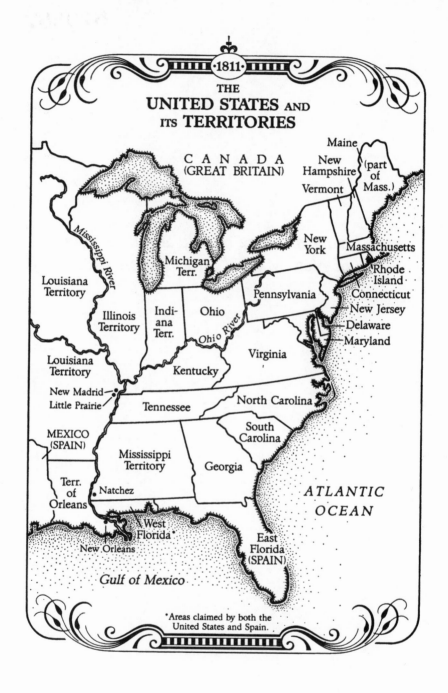

·1811·

THE
UNITED STATES AND
ITS TERRITORIES

CANADA
(GREAT BRITAIN)

Maine
New
Hampshire
Vermont
(part
of
Mass.)

New
York
Massachusetts

Louisiana
Territory

Michigan
Terr.

Pennsylvania

Rhode
Island
Connecticut
New Jersey
Delaware
Maryland

Illinois
Territory

Indi-
ana
Terr.

Ohio

Ohio River

Mississippi River

Louisiana
Territory

Kentucky

Virginia

New Madrid
Little Prairie

Tennessee

North Carolina

MEXICO
(SPAIN)

Mississippi
Territory

South
Carolina

Georgia

Terr.
of
Orleans

Natchez

New Orleans

West
Florida

East
Florida
(SPAIN)

ATLANTIC
OCEAN

Gulf of Mexico

*Areas claimed by both the
United States and Spain.

 PROLOGUE

*S*tanding in the yard beside their log house, Laurel looked at the starred December sky, quickly located the comet, and shivered—but from fear rather than the cold.

From the time eight years ago, in 1803, when America bought Louisiana, the vast area west of the Mississippi, from France, Father had wanted to leave Kentucky and move here, to New Madrid County. Last autumn, he had come alone and returned with a deed to fifty acres of land.

In March of this year of 1811, soon after she turned fifteen—at about the same time she first espied the comet—Laurel, her brother, Jedidiah, seventeen, and Mother and Father had put their belongings in the wagon and spread a tarpaulin over them. Father hitched the mules, Samson and Pretty Girl, to the wagon, and they set out for the Ohio River, forty miles away. Mother rode Father's horse, Galahad. Laurel,

Father, Jed, their part-collie dog, Ranger, the cow, Dolly, and the nameless brood sow walked. The large blue cat, Smoke, found a comfortable spot on the wagon tarp and looked out at them as if they were her subjects.

At the Ohio, they had loaded belongings and animals onto a flatboat and paid the haulage and their fares to the captain, who brought them down the Ohio to the Mississippi, then down and across the Mississippi to the City of New Madrid. Nearly two hundred people already lived there, and Father said it would become a big city, and he would be a farrier, one who shod and treated horses. In the meantime, they would farm the acreage he had bought west of town.

The previous owner had dug a well, felled some of the trees, and built the log house, which had a split-log floor rather than a dirt floor. And in addition to the area that served as Mother and Father's bedroom, living room, and kitchen, a loft afforded sleeping space for Laurel and Jed.

People came to welcome them and helped raise a barn with a corncrib, a hayloft, and—beneath the hayloft—an open space with a four-foot-wide door at the back. When it rained, the animals stood in the open space beneath the loft. With the arrival of winter, Father had opened the door so they could go inside the barn. Smoke, although received in the house to catch mice, also slept in the barn.

When all was done, the sow had a small sty and house of her own, and although it didn't have walls, the chickens had a two-foot-high roof over their heads at night. Ranger slept near the chickens, which would otherwise be easy prey for wild animals. A rail fence to deter large wild animals wound around the outbuildings, the lot, and a garden plot, but not the house because Mother said a fence would close out future neighbors. Game—from fish and rabbits to bear and deer—was plentiful, and Father had gone into town and bought winter supplies of rice, flour, cornmeal, dried beans, and other staples.

Their blessings were many, but something was terribly wrong. An army of squirrels was leaving, people said, running at such a pace that when one fell, those behind it trampled it to death. Enormous gars, catfish, and turtles had come up from the bottom of the river, and snakes had crawled out of their hibernation holes. Some said the creatures sensed that the comet was about to fall into the Ohio at the point where it flowed into the Mississippi, which would set in motion Earth's final days.

Laurel told herself that she placed no credence in such a prediction, but she had to acknowledge that since its appearance last March, the comet, with its head and double tail, had become ever larger, which surely meant it was closer. She shivered again and went back inside.

 CHAPTER 1

*L*aurel sat down at the desk, a prized posses-
sion Father had inherited, to write about
the waning day, the comet, and whatever
else came to mind. While she didn't make
an entry every day, she had kept a journal since she
had learned to write. She reached into the desk shelf
and took out her tablet and goose-feather quill. Repeated sharpening had shortened the quill, but the
point was blunt, and she should sharpen it again. No,
she would wait, make it last longer. She opened her
tablet and ink bottle.

Instead of writing, though, she looked around their
home, warmed by the hearth fire that added its glow
to the light from an oil lamp. It looked merry in here,

like Christmas, which was still ten days away. Sparks danced up the chimney, and garlands of small, dried red peppers hanging in the corner reflected the fire-glow. The glow became dim at the back of the big room, but she could see Mother and Father's bed and dresser. She was glad for Mother and Father's sake that all four of them didn't have to sleep in the same room, as they had in Kentucky. This house had a sleeping loft.

"Share with us," Mother said to her, and Jedidiah, who lay on his stomach on a bearskin rug in front of the fireplace, rolled over and sat up.

Laurel laughed. Jed was not much of a reader, but he did love a story, and she could tell a fair story. "I was thinking how merry everything looks," she said.

Jed grunted and lay back down, again on his stomach. This time he didn't look into the fire. His right elbow on the bearskin, his chin and jaw on his palm, his expression resentful, he watched Father. He used to idolize Father, but of late, his attitude had changed. And Father didn't help; he seemed to forget that Jed was a man grown. Mother said she thought that was the whole problem. Father wanted to maintain his authority, and Jed needed to assert his independence.

"Your mother has a knack for making a house a home," Father said without looking up from the rifle gun he was oiling and, Laurel knew, studying. He didn't measure the powder into a horn each time he

loaded. He put the ball and the right amount of powder into paper packets he folded together himself. He only had to open a packet, pour the ball-and-powder charge into the gun barrel bore, push it down with a rod, aim, pull back the hammer, and release it to strike the percussion cap that set off the charge. He believed, though, that there must be a way to make a breech-loading gun—that the ammunition should be placed behind the bore, not into it.

If so, Laurel thought as she entered the date—*December 15, 1811*—Father would figure out how to do it. In the eastern city of Philadelphia, where he had lived as a young man, he had gained many skills. He had most liked being a farrier. Ever restless, though, even after marrying Mother, he had wanted to move away from Philadelphia, then to move again and again. Mother said she thought that beginning with the Pilgrims, American men had a condition called "wandering feet."

Surely, Laurel thought, this move would be their last. Jed could look forward to a good life here, whatever he chose to do. And since a highly-regarded woman teacher operated a school in New Madrid, Mother and Father believed that despite Laurel's deformity—a harelip—she, too, could have a rewarding life here as a schoolteacher.

Father said that in Shropshire, Wales, where he was a child, people believed that a harelip came about

because a hare had crossed the path of the mother-to-be. But when Laurel was born in America, he said as much to the midwife, and she snorted and said that was bosh. She had seen harelips worse than this babe's, she said, and furthermore, the cleft palate that accompanied a harelip was the more serious. Fortunately, she said, this one's divided palate had almost closed before birth; she would have no trouble even with liquids if she drank slowly.

To Laurel, it didn't matter how they came to be, or which was more serious. She had, at age twelve, received heartbreaking information. No man, an older girl had told her, would ask Laurel to wed, for she did not have a kissable mouth.

When she was writing, though, her mind was too busy with the forming of words and sentences to think about a future without husband or children. She skipped down a line from the date and wrote:

*We have eaten a fine supper of squirrel and dumplings, and the house is cozy, but our animals are restless. I cannot but wonder if the comet, which glows ever brighter, is the cause. In addition to this natural marvel, a manmade one, the New Orleans, a Fulton steamboat built in Pittsburg, Pennsylvania, by Mr. Nicholas Roosevelt, will soon arrive in New Madrid.*

Last week Father and Jed had gone into town to buy meal and sugar and flour. When they returned home, they told Mother and Laurel that the steamboat had left Pittsburg on October twentieth and would already be here if Mrs. Roosevelt had not delivered Henry Latrobe, three-year-old Rosetta's little brother, on board the *New Orleans* at Louisville, Kentucky. The Roosevelts had decided to stay in Louisville for a while, and had done so until Sunday morning, December eighth.

"Only a few more days and the *New Orleans* will arrive in New Madrid," Laurel said. "You're sure, Jed, that your friend will send word the minute it's sighted upriver?"

"I'm sure," Jed said. "Roberto doesn't break promises."

Ah, yes, Laurel thought. Roberto. Jed's friend in town. A well-to-do man whose wife had died in childbirth, as had the baby. She and Mother and Father didn't go into town as often as Jed did, but once they had been with him and met Roberto. Roberto de Vega. Her heart had raced when he looked at her with those dark eyes and said that he was pleased to meet her.

Ranger whined outside the door, and a chill at the back of Laurel's neck raised the small hairs there. Ranger would not have left his post near the chickens' shelter without good reason. A fox? He wouldn't

hesitate to attack a fox. And although he would stay out of a bear's reach, bears did not intimidate him. Indians? Few Indians lived in and around New Madrid, and those who did were friendly, not like the Indians in Kentucky. A lynx or panther maybe. Ranger was afraid of wild cats. But why would either leave a woods bountiful with small game even in December and come to a place with dog and human smell? A skunk? Skunks loved eggs, and Ranger had once challenged a skunk. Yes, a skunk would make him beg to come inside.

Father put on his deerskin jacket, which Laurel knew already had the ammunition packets in a pocket, picked up the gun and rod, and went out. Mother continued to sew, but her body had tensed. Jed stood and paced. Like Father, Jed felt responsible for their welfare, but without Father's bidding, he could only wait, as she and Mother waited. She would write down the things that had gone through her mind. She started to dip the quill in the ink, and instead, gazed at the bottle. How strange. The ink was moving.

She looked up as Father came back inside, set the gun in its corner, and removed his jacket. "I saw nothing and heard nothing," he said.

She had been considering something . . . the ink. The ink was quite still.

"Whatever is bothering them was probably also listening and watching," Jed said.

Quietly, speaking to Mother, but giving what Laurel knew was a warning to Jed to mind his tongue, Father said, "Nor did I sense the presence of person or wild creature."

Mother, her face calm in her relief, said, "Then there is nothing there."

"Two of the chickens were off the roost and lying on their backs," Father said. "I returned them to the roost."

Mother frowned. "But a chicken does not fall legs up, nor turn onto its back."

Laurel almost laughed. Mother knew that, too. When Laurel was little, she had heard an old man say he was as helpless as a chicken on its back. She had tried pushing a hen over with a stick, and when it managed to dodge the stick, she had grabbed the hen and placed it on its back. There the poor thing, eyes rolling, had lain until she set it aright. She had been ashamed and considered confessing her wickedness to Mother, who had evidently made the same experiment.

"Bedtime!" Mother said firmly, and Jed, who always went up to the loft and to bed before Laurel did, immediately rose and bade them goodnight.

# CHAPTER 2

*A*s Jed went up the steps, Laurel looked at the mantel clock. Five minutes after nine. She could follow Jed's movements from the sounds: he had reached the loft; he was undressing. He had retired. In the quiet, she could hear the animals outside still restlessly moving about.

She put away the quill, ink, and her tablet; brushed her hair; said goodnight to Mother and Father; and went up the steep, narrow steps to the loft. Good, Jed was not asleep. He often fell asleep so quickly that it aggravated her. She liked to talk a bit. She changed into her nightgown, silently said her evening prayers, lay down on her narrow hen-feather mattress, and

pulled up the covers. "You're wide awake, too," she said in a low voice. "And the animals are restless. Do you think it's because of the comet? Or maybe we're about to have falling weather."

Jed sighed. "It's not the weather or the comet that's made me restless, Laur. I'm afraid I'm in love."

She drew in a quiet breath but only waited. If she pushed Jed, he might turn stubborn and say nothing.

"I probably don't have a chance," Jed said. "She's beautiful. Catherine—Catherine LaBrix—is not like other girls I've met. She's really shy, but it doesn't matter because she says it all with her eyes."

"How did you meet her?" Laurel asked, as if she were making light talk.

"Roberto introduced her to me. Actually, I think she's kind of smitten with Roberto, but he's not interested in her, so the field is clear."

While Laurel considered what to ask next, Jed's breathing became slow and even. He had always done this, gone to sleep when she would like to talk. At least she knew his friend Roberto was not also interested in the beautiful girl who had unsettled Jed's heart. She turned over; closed her eyes; took calm, even breaths; and felt herself drifting down toward sleep.

Her eyes opened suddenly. A cold draft sent a chill through her. The door had been opened; Father must still be concerned about the animals.

After about ten minutes, he came back inside and returned to his bed. He said something to Mother, but Laurel could not make out the words. Then all was quiet. She had gone into sleep, albeit uneasy sleep, when thunder brought her back to awakeness and the drowsy thought that now she had not only to worry about the comet's falling, but about thunder rumbling up from the ground instead of down from the sky. Her eyes opened wide; she stared into blackness stabbed with flickers of light from the banked hearth fire below.

Thunder from ground instead of sky. Nervous animals. Upside-down chickens. Not the comet. Earth. Earthquake! Father liked history; he had told Jed and her about the great Lisbon, Portugal, earthquake of 1755. She scrambled off the mattress.

"Jed! Laurel!" Father shouted. "Throw down your covers. And your clothes. Earthquake. Quickly! Quickly!"

Her heart pounding so hard it jarred her chest, Laurel tossed things downstairs. Blanket. Dresses. Undergarments. Shoes. Jed, wheezing as if he could not get enough air, did the same. Inside a roar like that of a mighty wind, she left the loft first; when she reached the floor, she fell to her knees. Jed, immediately behind her, helped her stand. The door stood wide open. Shaking from fear and the cold air, she gagged from a gaseous, nauseating stench.

Beneath the fireplace ashes, banked coals glowed. The lamp was not on the table. Of course not; Father would have immediately set it outside lest it fall and break, and set the house afire. Ranger was sitting beneath the table; she heard his nervous panting and smelled him. His smell always became strong when he was frightened.

Not only did the door stand open, Father had punched out the hide from one of the windows, and while Mother tossed things through it, he pitched other belongings through the door. "Take the clock as you go, Jed," Mother said, and at the same time, Father said, "The coals, Jed!" and Mother said, "Never mind the clock." Jed's hands shook as he shoveled embers into the ash bucket. Laurel picked up the mantel clock; it was three minutes past two. Her cloak and bonnet! Not on their pegs; Mother and Father had already put them and her wool shawl outside.

The split-log floor teetered; Laurel almost fell, and dropped the clock. She heard the glass shatter at the same time Father yelled, "Outside! Now!"

Ranger realized they were leaving, ran from beneath the table, and almost knocked her down in his determination to stay with them.

They were in the yard; Father gave precise orders: *"Get away from the house. Sit down. Draw up your knees."*

Rumbling thunder rolled around them; lightning

flashed; and Laurel's scalp crawled as if it were trying to escape her head because the thunder and lightning came up from the ground instead of down from the sky. A dull roar engulfed her; the ground moved upward, then plunged downward. From near and far, animals—pigs, cattle, horses, foxes, wildcats, panthers, and wolves—screamed in terror. As did crows and sparrows and other birds that stayed in winter. Birds were supposed to sing, or chirp, or caw during daylight hours; she had never heard them in the night, nor known that they could scream.

The cabin logs strained against each other; pieces of the chimney hit the ground with heavy thuds. The high-pitched cracking of tree branches and trunks rode on the roar. A far-off bell clanged.

The noise subsided; the ground stopped its terrible heaving. She would stroke it with gratitude, Laurel thought, if not for the noxious odor rising from it.

"The smell is that of sulfur," Father said.

"We should have come straight outside," Jed said in a trembling, accusing voice. "We're lucky the house didn't fall on us."

Now Jed was faulting Father!

"We were right to bring out supplies, Son," Father said. His earlier flaring impatience was not there; he only sounded tired.

Laurel still trembled; her heart still beat hard and fast. "It's cold," she said, and saying it gave her body

a familiar problem with which to contend. Her heart-beat slowed and the trembling bated. Either her sight had adjusted, or the darkness had lessened. The barn had not fallen. The toilet was a pile of wood, but the smokehouse and springhouse were also still standing. "I hope others fared as well as we," she said, and the springhouse fell in a heap.

"The worst may be yet to come," Father said. He stood then, helped Mother to her feet, and said to Jed, "Make a small fire. We cannot go back inside. The house is surely weakened."

The ground moved again; they all immediately dropped back to the ground and curled up, but this shaking was like an echo compared to the first one. Father stood and said, "I'm going to check on the animals."

They stood, too, and Ranger, panting hard, neither trotted ahead of Father nor walked to heel; he stayed so close to Father's right leg that Laurel feared Father would trip over him. Smoke! Where was Mother's cat?

Mother looked toward the deep woods and Laurel wanted to say, "Don't worry. Smoke will come back." But she couldn't; she didn't understand cats either. She took a step and almost fell. Mother took her hand and they went to watch Jed build the fire.

# CHAPTER 3

**F**ather veered from the lot gate path to check the chickens' shelter. "Gone," he said in a raised voice. "All of them." Mother moaned.

Before he reached the lot, the brood sow came to Mother and Jed and Laurel, grunting in an excited voice. "I know, dear, but it's over now," Mother said to the brood sow. Laurel watched the black forms, even darker than the night: Father, with Ranger walking beside him, now at the gate; Galahad, snorting in terror, on the other side of it. Father opened the gate for Galahad to come outside, rubbed the great horse's nose, and patted his neck. "Stay," he then said to Ranger. He went inside the lot and reclosed the gate.

For once, Laurel thought, Father was so rattled he had done something from habit. With the brood sow outside the lot before he opened the gate, some of the fencing had to be down. So why close the gate? He slowly moved deeper into the lot; blackness swallowed him. Of course! Father couldn't simply command Galahad to stay as he did Ranger. Galahad would walk behind him. If Galahad stepped into an earth crack... Laurel shuddered.

Ranger watched intently, his muscles taut, and she knew that with his superior night vision, he could still see Father. Ranger's tail wagged; a little later Father came out of the darkness enough that she could tell he was carrying Galahad's halter. He opened the gate, came into the yard, put the halter on Galahad, and dropped the guide rope so that it hung loose below Galahad's muzzle. He rubbed his hand over Ranger's head. "Sorry, boy, but you're on guard," he said. "Stay." He again went into the lot and closed the gate behind him; Ranger again stood peering through the slats. But Galahad relaxed, rippled his muscles, and walked a little way.

Laurel shook her head in awe. Wearing his halter, Galahad felt secure: experience told him Father was nearby, that he could move around but should go no more than a few feet in any direction.

"Your father's checking on the other animals," Mother said.

Mother knew she and Jed knew that, Laurel thought, but needed to say it because she was so worried about Dolly.

The earth shook; Laurel's heart beat faster. The earth became still; her heartbeat slowed. Where was the bloomin' moon?! It was bad enough for the sulfurous fog to cloak the stars and the comet, but even if it did not, they didn't lend light. She bit her bottom lip to keep from giggling; if she started, she might not be able to stop. They had been through an earthquake and were unharmed. But she wished for the moon!

Ranger still stood looking between the gate slats into the darkness. Jed's fire spread a soft glow, but it went only so far, and as Laurel looked beyond the glow's rim, she saw—west of them, just inside the black wall of night—two pairs of orange-tinted yellow eyes, animals' eyes reflecting the firelight. She shuddered. Wolves. She all but prayed that between the intensity of his waiting and the pungent lot smells, Ranger would not catch their scent. If he were alone, he would ignore them as long as they didn't come too close, but he was not alone. And in his keyed-up state, if he realized the wolves were there, he would feel that he must protect his humans and attack. Laurel put her hand on Jed's arm and tilted her head to indicate the wolves' location.

Mother realized that something more than the earth's shudders had claimed their attention and

turned her head to also look. She nodded but did not speak. Jed, his face set, took a stick out of the fire and, walking toward the wolves, swung it in an arc. The glowing stick flared; the wolves trotted away, silently melding with the night.

Still intently watching, Ranger wagged his tail, which meant Father was coming toward the gate. Jed returned and laid the burning stick back into the fire pit. Father came out of the gate. He spoke to Galahad and patted his neck, but didn't remove the halter. Father then rubbed Ranger's head, praised him, and, with Ranger beside him, came to join them. "Some sections of the fence are down," he said, and gave a heavy sigh. "Dolly's gone. So are Samson and Pretty Girl."

Creatures had an affinity with earth that humans did not have, Laurel thought. When Father had gone out last evening to see if he could determine what was disturbing the animals, they had obviously already known something was wrong. The mules would return; they would remember that here they didn't have to search for food and fresh water. If Dolly had gone far, though, she wouldn't be able to find her way home. As to whether the rooster and the hens would come back, she had no idea.

Apparently a tremor neither people nor animals had detected had caused the hens to turn on their backs last evening. Last evening, she had written *December 15.* They were now well into December sixteenth. Maybe

the chickens had found safety somewhere. In Kentucky their chickens had made it up into a young maple the time a fox decided he was in the mood for a chicken dinner. That was probably it; they were roosting in a tree.

"Bedtime!" Mother said.

It seemed as if days rather than hours had passed since Mother last said those words.

Although their bodies would lend warmth to one another if they lay on blankets and spread blankets over them, they had learned during their various moves that it was better to lie separately. Otherwise, either Father on one side or Jed on the other would in sleep reposition self and disturb the covers. They therefore individually, and with space between them, rolled themselves in a blanket: Father, Mother, Laurel, Jed. Together they said the Lord's Prayer. Then all was quiet.

Another shudder, harder than the last several, went through the ground. More of the chimney fell, and Laurel's breathing quickened. The shaking only lasted a few seconds. Her breathing slowed, but fear and a sense of helplessness made her throat ache.

The stars still looked as if they were behind a gauzy curtain, but she could see them. And there was the comet, dim, but still there. That the comet had not fallen comforted her, and she began to fall asleep. The earth trembled; she returned to heart-thudding awakeness. Even in fantasy, she could not count sheep lightly bounding one by one over a fence. Stars. She would count the dim stars.

# CHAPTER 4

*G*alahad's whinnying and a sound like faraway thunder brought Laurel to the edge of awakening. She shifted her body, came awake although she didn't open her eyes, and knew she had to rise. She couldn't; she had never been this weary. She had finally fallen into exhausted sleep despite the small quakes that followed the big one at two o'clock, but another strong one had awakened them near dawn.

She didn't have a choice; she had to get up. But doing so without disturbing Jed on one side of her and Mother on the other presented a problem. She wriggled out of her blanket roll, stood, and stretched. The lightening of the winter sky told her it was going on

seven o'clock.  Not that it mattered, except she liked to know the time.

Banked coals blinking through the ashes supplied scarce warmth; she shivered, quickly pulled on her stockings and shoes, picked up her shawl from atop the log she had sat on last night, put it across her shoulders, and stood.

Galahad whinnied again.  He still stood near the gate, but in a strange position—his head hanging low, his legs spread wide.

Laurel pulled her shawl more snugly around her and started toward the crippled woods on yonder side of the road that ran in front of the house.  She had only gone a dozen or so steps when the earth shook, and shook harder still, and there was no longer need to reach the woods.  She had to get back to her family.  In turning around, she fell.  On her hands and knees, she began to crawl.  The earth shook violently.  She fell flat on her stomach.

The shaking suddenly ceased; she got back to her hands and knees, but now the ground began to roll in waves.  Earth waves around her loudly exploded.  When they burst they spewed sand and black chunks of what looked like charcoal.  What if one burst directly beneath her?  Her muscles went limp from fear of death; her bones seemed to dissolve.  She lay curled on her side, her hands over her ears.  Creatures screeched and screamed and howled in chorus with the clatters

and crashing of trees and planks, and a roaring wind tossed the explosion sounds one way, then another. The stench of sulfur filled her nostrils; her diaphragm spasmed; bile burned her throat.

She managed to get back to her hands and knees, vomited the meager amount of undigested food in her stomach, then retched and retched again. She collapsed and lay prone, and her urine-wet garments set her to shaking with a terrible coldness.

Galahad screamed. He was still screaming when the rolling and the roar stopped, and the waves became ripples. Laurel again got to her hands and knees and turned until he was in her line of vision. Hysterically thrashing, Galahad lay in the yard near the fence—or what had been the fence. It was now a tangle of sticks in strange formations. Father, on his elbows and stomach, and holding his rifle gun, wriggled toward Galahad. By the time Father reached him, the earth had become quite calm, and Jed stood and walked to them.

Father handed his gun and an ammunition packet up to Jed. She didn't need to hear Father to know he was patting Galahad and talking in a low, soothing voice. The whinnying ceased, the thrashing stopped, and Father moved his hands over one, then another of Galahad's legs, until he had checked all four.

Father stood but did not take the gun from Jed. Laurel let out a shuddering sigh. She couldn't hear him, but she knew Father continued to talk quietly,

and at last the big horse got to his feet, shook his head, and snorted. He still trembled; she could see the ripples.

Father took hold of the rein he had put on Galahad last night to make him feel secure and coaxed him to take a step. And another step. The trembling eased; Galahad limped, but it was not a bad limp. They stopped walking; Father patted Galahad's neck, and although she couldn't hear him, she knew Father was assuring Galahad that he would be fine, that his hurt leg was only bruised. Horses, Laurel knew, especially fine horses like Galahad, were not bright. They were, in fact, dumb. But they knew their legs were vulnerable, and perhaps knew that breaking one meant certain death. Therefore, pain in one of their legs thrust them into panic.

Galahad's shivering ceased; he snorted, shook his great body and tossed his head, nudged Father with his nose, then gazed eastward as if he longed to be back in Kentucky.

Laurel stood. Mother came and embraced her, and Laurel burst into tears. Mother, crying too, smoothed her hair. "It's all right, darling," she said. "Shh, hush now."

"The waves . . . " Laurel said, and giggled although tears still ran down her face. "I wet myself."

"Small wonder!" Mother said, and her witticism sent them into a spate of giggles. When they bated,

Mother said, "I'll get a pan and a pitcher of warm water while you fetch dry undergarments and a dress."

"Yes, ma'am," Laurel said. As she went for the clothes, she took note of the damage. The springhouse and toilet were pieces of wood, some planks in stacks, others tossed here and there. The barn had collapsed. The house still stood, but most of the chimney had crumbled.

When they had the clothing and the pitcher of bathing water, she and Mother went to the front of the house. "Rice," Mother said as if Laurel had asked aloud about breakfast. "But there won't be any butter to put on it, nor milk to put over it." She sighed, and as she turned to go wash and cook the rice, which would take ages—around forty minutes—she said, "Oh, I do hope Dolly is all right."

She was glad Mother had left, Laurel thought as she took off her shawl, folded it, and laid it aside. Her face surely revealed her doubt that their docile, sweet-smelling cow was still alive.

West of them, the woods didn't look as torn and tangled as they did on the east side, toward town and the river. In that direction, many trees were down. The roots of an enormous elm made her think of a grotesque monster. Near it, the limbs of two partially uprooted cottonwoods leaned into each other like embracing lovers.

She removed her dress and, shivering, loosely folded

it and laid it atop her shawl. Now for her thin old petticoat. What if someone came along the road? The quakes had addled her brain. They lived, as the saying went, "at the end of the road," and going eastward, toward New Madrid and the river, there were no other houses until you neared town.

She bent down to take hold of the hem of her petticoat and peel it over her head. A throat-clearing sound stopped her. She straightened up and knew from the warmth that rushed into her that she was blushing from head to foot. Jed's friend Roberto de Vega was walking beside Dolly along the ruptured, wagon-wide road, loosely holding a rope tied around her neck. Even cows knew the way home if someone accompanied them lest they ramble off the road and forget where they were going.

Dolly turned into the yard. Mr. Vega, who had pulled back his shining black hair and tied it with a piece of red yarn, made no effort to look at sky or ground; he looked at Laurel and made a slight bow as he continued to walk. He was not handsome, but he did have magnetism. And while she had heard females make much of a man's height, a robust body was to her a more important physical attribute. About five feet, six inches tall, he could, with those arms and shoulders, pull a willow sapling from the ground as if it were a cocklebur.

He went on toward the back of the house and out of

view; Laurel quickly removed her undergarments, lifted the pitcher to her neck, tilted the spout downward, and poured the water down her front, sides, and back. Shaking hard, she set down the pitcher, picked up the towel, and began to dry herself.

Ranger's low, menacing growl came from the backyard; she paused in her toweling and sucked in her breath. She should have warned their benefactor. Father was back there; she need not worry. Even in his wrought-up state, Ranger wouldn't attack unless Father bade him to. Quickly, she put on her undergarments. Mr. Vega had one of their animals!

"Good morning, Jed," he said in a raised voice. "Stay your dog, please."

In surprised response, Jed said, "Roberto?" Then, happily, "Roberto! How in the world . . . ? Ranger, come!"

Laurel let out a relieved breath, pulled on her dress, and settled her shawl around her. Mercy, she was cold. So, if she came down with pneumonia she would at least be clean when the doctor came.

"Dolly!" Mother said. "Isn't it wonderful, dear? Mr. Vega has brought Dolly home."

Laurel all but laughed aloud. Mother had just warned Father to be more than coolly polite to their visitor and benefactor even though he was Spanish. In Father's mind, the Spanish thought New Madrid still belonged to them, and furthermore, the wicked

Spanish, like the wicked French, enjoyed wine and dancing.

The wood smoke smelled wonderful. And although she didn't drink coffee, even it smelled good. Her face would turn pink; Mother, and perhaps Father and Jed, would know that Mr. Vega had seen her when she was not fully clothed. A warm fire burned back there. Laurel raised her chin and went to join her family and Roberto de Vega.

 CHAPTER 5

*L*aurel had almost reached the fire circle, her family, and their visitor when another shock hit. She immediately sat down, flat on the ground. Mother did the same, then grabbed the rod-lift; positioned it beneath the pot's wire handle; removed the pot lest it turn over, spill the rice, and douse the fire; and set it in what Laurel supposed one would call a "pot pen"—four short lengths of small, split logs Father had laid on their flat sides in a square outside the fire circle.

Dolly bawled once, and only once, as if to say, "Enough!"

When the ground became steady again, Mother returned the rice pot to the coals, stood, and brushed

the back of her dress. Laurel also stood and, her chin high, went on to join the others.

Mother's face questioned, and Laurel lifted her dress slightly so Mother could see her petticoat and therefore know she had not been in a state of complete undress.

"Do stay for breakfast, Mr. Vega," Mother said.

"Thank you, Señora Mawston," he said. "It will be my pleasure to share breakfast."

"Laurel, dear," Mother, her eyes fairly dancing, said as she poured some water from the kettle into the milk pail, "would you keep an eye on the rice. I must milk poor Dolly." She dipped the back of her hand into the water to be sure it was neither too hot nor too cold.

She would, Laurel knew, serve herself ill to glare at Mother, but she did send a mental message: *Most mothers would be upset if they knew a strange man had seen their daughter in her petticoat, but my mother thinks it's funny!*

Mother smiled at her and went to Dolly while Jed fetched the milking stool. Crooning, Mother washed Dolly's swollen udder and teats and began. The streams of milk made pinging music as they hit the bottom of the pail.

Laurel put the sugar bowl on a flat stone, gathered bowls and spoons, and tried not to look at Roberto. He looked at her on occasion, though; she knew because her face would become warm and without thinking, she would bring her right index finger and its

neighbor to the center of her top lip to cover the split there. Once he willed her to meet his eyes. Her heart beat faster, and she decided that she must say something lest he think she not only had the harelip, but that she had lost her ability to speak. "Tecumseh's Comet has been bright of late, until last night," she said.

"Yes," Roberto said.

She jerked her eyes away from his and covered her mouth with her fingers. What did the comet's being bright have to do with anything?! He probably thought she had another affliction—that she was a blooming idiot.

When Mother finished milking, they ate with little talk because it was ill-mannered to speak of unpleasant things while eating, but when they had set their bowls aside, and Mother had refilled the coffee cups, Father asked how the quakes had affected New Madrid.

"It is very bad," Roberto said. "In the town, people are living in tents. Mrs. LaBeck died from a heart attack. John Luther Griggs suffered a broken leg. At the cove, many boats were damaged. Some of the animals on the boats—horses, pigs, and cows—drowned, but no men, I am told. Fortunately, most had come ashore for a night of merrymaking."

"Mr. Griggs' leg?" Jed said. "Was it a bad break?"

Roberto nodded.

Laurel moaned. She well understood the meaning of

the dreaded words "bad break." The bone had pene-
trated the flesh, which meant that Mr. Griggs' leg had
to be sawed off above the break. She hoped he was not
one of those people who would not drink whiskey no
matter what, and that a plentiful supply had been available.

Roberto's silence continued; Laurel and her family
waited. He might not want to talk further about the
earthquake, or he might need to talk.

"Children cry," he said at last. "Old ones shake."

Mother looked toward the woods, and in a low voice
quoted a saying: "I wept because I had no shoes until I
met a man who had no feet."

Perhaps, Laurel thought, she would someday explain
to Roberto about Mother's cat, Smoke, but not now.

They were silent for a time, then Father asked,
"Were the quakes widespread?"

Roberto nodded and set down his coffee cup.
"Chickasaws say no place for many miles either upriver
or downriver has been spared."

Laurel had heard it said that with their swift canoes,
the Chickasaws could gather or deliver information
downriver or upriver while white people were still dis-
cussing how to word the message they would send via
a runner.

"Where did you grow up, Mr. Vega?" Mother asked,
and Laurel lowered her head so he couldn't see her
face. He didn't know it, but he was about to divulge a

lot more than his birthplace. Mother was truly interested in people and had a unique skill when it came to
learning about them.

He had grown up in New Orleans. During his fif-
teenth year, his parents had died within months of
each other. He had joined a keelboat crew, and after a
few trips to New Madrid, decided to live there. He
had trapped on the Missouri for a time, then stopped
trapping, become a fur trader, and built a home in
New Madrid.

When Roberto said a little later that he must go, he
seemed to debate with himself as to whether he should
tell something else. "Chickasaws say the steamboat is
still coming," he said. "It is due December nineteenth."

Two days hence! The *New Orleans* would reach
New Madrid sometime Thursday. Jed's face glowed
with excitement—and while a boat propelled by steam
rather than muscle power did not intrigue Laurel as
much as it did him, she would like to see it, and to
meet Mrs. Roosevelt.

Roberto again thanked Mother for the breakfast and
bade them farewell. Jed stepped up beside Roberto to
walk a way with him, but Father said, "Son, I'd like to
have a word with Mr. Vega."

The request startled Laurel and, she could tell, Jed.
Father and Roberto walked beyond her and Jed's hearing
distance. After a brief conversation, they shook

hands. Father had likely only thanked Roberto again for bringing Dolly home.

Upon his return from walking a way with Roberto, Jed said that as you went eastward the trembling was harder than here, and the earth rents wider and deeper—and that there were sand blows, bubbling mud, and smells worse than the sulfur odor.

Laurel shuddered. Roberto lived farther eastward than Jed had walked.

 CHAPTER 6

*S*amson and Pretty Girl, looking no worse for their adventure except for dried cockleburs in their tails, returned no more than an hour after Roberto's departure. They went straight to the lot gate, and when Father did not go immediately to open it, Samson turned his head and looked at him as if he were neglectful of his duties to them.

"I gather," said Mother, "that mules are like people—creatures of habit."

Father laughed, which he did not often do, and Laurel knew that while he had insisted that they would return, doubt had pestered him. "If their majesties entered at any place other than the gate, they would have to walk across downed rails and posts," he said.

He went to the gate, opened it, and bowed as the mules trudged past Galahad into the lot.

When he came back, he spoke directly to Jed. "Maybe we ought to repair the fence."

Laurel looked from Father to Jed. Yes, Jed realized that Father had spoken to him differently, as able man rather than bumbling child. She sighed. If only she could help mend the fence. If only she had something to do. If only the earth would stop its incessant trembling! The rhythm itself had become maddening: Shake. Wait. Shake. Maybe if she could stop thinking about Roberto, her foolish heart would stop trembling!

"Of course," Father said glumly, "there's not much point in trying to repair the fence until the shaking stops."

"You ever known Samson and Pretty Girl to make the same mistake twice?" Jed asked, and after a startled moment, Father laughed. "You're right," he said. "You're absolutely right. If the entire fence falls down, they'll pretend not to notice."

As terrible as they were, Laurel thought, even earthquakes did something good.

The shaking eased as the day waned, and they slept reasonably well that night.

In late afternoon of the next day, December seventeenth, Mother—who didn't know the meaning of the words "give up"—shelled corn and called, "Here,

chick. Chick, chick." And from the ragged woods came five chickens with red and rolling eyes that made them look demented. The way they walked made them appear more so. They raised one foot, moved it forward, swayed, brought it to the ground, stood for a moment, then brought up the other foot and repeated the procedure. Mother's eyes filled with tears. "Poor things," she said, and Laurel all but laughed aloud. Mother could expertly wring a chicken's neck.

Twilight came, and with it, further easing of the tremors. Evening gave way to night. The sulfur smell had gone. Stars bloomed, which surely meant the haze was also gone, a good sign, Laurel thought. They said their prayers. Night deepened. They located the evening star, identified constellations, and noted the comet.

The ground, which had been still for what seemed a long time, shook, and Laurel hit it with her fist.

A few quiet minutes passed. Then, in her sweet soprano, Mother began to sing the second verse of "The Spacious Firmament." The first verse gave thanks for the day, the second for the night:

> *Soon as the evening shades prevail,*
> *The moon takes up the wondrous tale;*
> *And nightly to the listening earth*
> *Repeats the story of her birth;*
> *Whilst all the stars that round her burn,*

*And all the planets in their turn,*
*Confirm the tidings as they roll,*
*And spread the truth from pole to pole.*

Tears seeped from beneath Laurel's closed eyelids. Listening earth. Poor suffering earth. And she had hit it with her fist and blamed it for their misery. She had best be honest; she had blamed it for *her* misery.

At last—and it was still a night sky, not a sky heralding dawn—she went to sleep despite the occasional tremors, which had become milder and less frequent. When she awakened to aging morning, she lay still, listening, wondering what was wrong. Birds. Sparrows chirping. Nothing was wrong! She sat up and was about to awaken her family to share the joyful news when the earth shook again and the sparrows hushed their voices.

A short time later, though, she knew for certain that the shocks that had followed the two great earthquakes had lessened in frequency and intensity. She looked at the sky—a pale blue winter sky—on that morning of December eighteenth, 1811, and murmured, "Thank you."

 CHAPTER 7

*M*other and Father were up and stirring about; Jed sat up, yawned, and rubbed his fingers beneath his nose. He shook his head as if to clear it. Watching him, Laurel smiled.

"Do I hear birds?" Jed asked. "Or have the quakes addled my brain?"

"I fear it is only a respite," Father said.

"A respite long enough for you and me to go rabbit hunting?"

Laurel all but gasped; Jed had taken the lead.

Father laughed and said, "How does stewed rabbit sound to you, Mother?"

Laurel took in a deep breath of the cold, crisp

morning air. Early morning or early evening, when rabbits came out of their burrows to feed, was the best time to find them. Or rather, it was that way ordinarily. The earthquakes might have destroyed the burrows.

"Stewed rabbit sounds good," Mother said. "And we brought out flour. We'll have stewed rabbit and dumplings."

Laurel put on her shoes, wrapped her shawl around her, picked up the near-empty water bucket, and walked away from her family to the front yard, across the road, and into the crippled woods. She wished *she* could go rabbit hunting. She went to a stream flowing to the river and filled the bucket. She wished she had any kind of diversion!

The ground moved. "I didn't mean it!" she said sharply. Toting the water back from the stream, she studied the house. It leaned, and part of the chimney had crumbled, but if she moved slowly and softly, she could surely go inside and bring out a few more things, the ink and her writing tablet among them.

Father and Jed had not yet left when she reached the yard. "Father," she said, "I was wondering if. . . "

"No," he said. "You may not enter the house. Let's go, Jed."

They were gone for little more than an hour. They brought only four rabbits, not because they could not have killed more, but because they needed no more.

The day seemed to drag on forever. Once Laurel picked up a dirt clod, threw it at a red squirrel, and yelled, "Stop your silly fussing!"

"Laurel!" Mother said, and Father, currying Galahad, looked at her with astonishment.

"I'm sorry," Laurel said. "It's just that. . . " She would not cry. She would not.

Mother came to her and said, "Close your eyes, hold your chin high, and take a deep breath."

It worked. She felt better.

In midafternoon, they were all sitting around the fire when Ranger stood and growled. He didn't move; since Father was there, Ranger had to await his command. Noting Ranger's taut muscles, his readiness to attack even if he were completely outmatched, Laurel's own muscles tightened and a chill went down her spine. Seconds later a man of average height with very black skin hailed from the road. He sat astride a sleek, auburn mule outfitted with a bridle and a thick piece of cotton sacking that served as a saddle—all one needed to ride a mule. He stopped the mule beside a tall cottonwood stump on yonder side of the road.

Father bade Ranger to stay and went to greet the man, who dismounted and walked across the road to meet Father. "Señor Mawston?" he said.

Father nodded. "Yes."

"I am Tomas. I bring a message from Señor Vega. He regrets he could not come himself. He is helping

boatmen in the cove."

Laurel's heart beat harder and faster.

"The steamboat *New Orleans* will arrive in New Madrid tomorrow, December nineteenth. O'clock time is not known."

"I send a return message," Father said. "Jedidiah and Laurel Mawston will be in New Madrid early tomorrow. And thank you, Tomas."

"You are welcome," Tomas said. He went back to the mule, took hold of the bridle rope, turned the mule around, stepped upon the stump, mounted, and rode away without a backward glance.

Only then did Father's return message truly register. Laurel gasped and shook her head. She would not leave him and Mother. And neither would Jed.

 CHAPTER 8

*F*ather sat down on the same log with Mother, about six inches from her. Facing them, Laurel and Jed sat on another log. Laurel had become so used to the earth quivers that she paid scarce attention when one passed beneath the log. Father cleared his throat. "Mother and I have made our decision," he said. "We cannot leave on the steamboat. We have responsibilities to dependent creatures." He looked at Jed and her in turn, then said, "But you will go."

Laurel shook her head and opened her mouth to protest, but Father turned his palm toward her, and she kept her silence.

"Mother's aunt Martha and her good husband,

your great uncle John McKay, live in Natchez in Mississippi Territory," he said. "The steamboat will reach there before it arrives at the city of New Orleans. Natchez is an established town and, I have heard river men say, a sizeable one. Captain Roosevelt will no doubt stop there as a matter of course, but when you go aboard, Jed, immediately tell him that is where you wish to disembark, and ask him as to the fare."

Father cleared his throat and looked at her. "Laurel, commit the sum to memory along with information as to where we are to send payment, and write it down at your first opportunity." He gave them a few seconds to absorb those instructions, then said, "You will take most of what money we have, which Mother fortunately remembered to get when the first quake struck, but you must keep that in case some misfortune befalls you."

He fell silent, and Laurel carefully did not look at Jed, who finally said, "Yes, sir."

Laurel nodded, looked down, then tightly closed her eyes. Even so, tears escaped.

"In due time," Mother said, "we will be together again. Meanwhile . . . " Her voice faltered, but after a moment she continued, "it will comfort us to know you are safe."

"And now," Father said, "you have things to do."

Laurel dutifully—and after a while, with excitement

that she was going into town—made ready for the morrow. She hung her wool cape on the clothesline so the wrinkles would fall out. They heated water from the stream, and she and Jed bathed. Wrapped in blankets, they sat on a log beside the fire while Mother washed the garments they had been wearing, shook them briskly to get out as many wrinkles as possible, and hung them on the line to dry.

Mother served the leftover rabbit and dumplings; they ate without talking. It was not silent, of course. The bare trees spoke of their distress with low moans. A chunk of the chimney hit the ground with a thud. The fire noisily spat out a small piece of glowing wood. A dog's bark came so clearly through the night that Ranger lifted his head and listened intently for a few seconds, until he decided the bark did not concern him.

After their prayers and goodnights, Laurel lay on her side, staring into the darkness. There was no point in trying to fall asleep; her fancy took her to the morrow. She and Jed and others—including Roberto—stood on the bank, waiting for the steamboat. They were boarding now, and there was Mrs. Roosevelt, a charming lady with a warm smile. Captain Roosevelt had a full beard and a somewhat gruff voice to cover his true warm nature.

When they were underway, Laurel settled down on one knee and told little Rosetta she remembered how it

had hurt her neck to look way up to the giants' faces. During the long trip, Mrs. Roosevelt came to depend on her and asked her to rock Henry and play games with Rosetta. Jed liked to walk on deck and discuss with other men the faults and frailties of various political leaders. It would all be wonderful and exciting except that she knew how much Mother and Father missed Jed and her. Mother had already lost Smoke, and now her beloved children were also gone and she was bereft.

Laurel's eyes became wet, and she needed to blow her nose. How terribly sad it was to leave one's parents. Except for the time when they lived in Kentucky and she spent the night with Pauline Spriggs, she had never been away from them at night. Besides, she had just met Roberto.

The earth shook harder than it had at any time during the day. Dolly bawled a protest. Laurel turned in her blanket. This was going to be a long, miserable night; it would be impossible to go to sleep.

When Father shook her shoulder and told her it was time to rise and dress and go to the river lest the steamboat arrive early, she scrunched deeper into her blanket and sent him the thought for which she could not muster voice: *I just went to sleep and cannot get up.*

"Wake up, Laurel!" Father said, and this time his voice was stern.

The rising sun spread its light as she and Jed said their good-byes to Ranger in particular and the other animals in general, exchanged farewell hugs with Mother and Father, and set out for the river.

 CHAPTER 9

*W*alking along the animal-trodden dirt road, Laurel and Jed stepped over earth rents and dodged frost-dead weeds. The early-morning sun lent no warmth; her wool cape no more kept out the cold than her shoes blocked the ground quivers. She shifted her clothing bundle from one hand to the other and asked, "Do you really want to go on the *New Orleans?*"

"Sure," Jed said. "But I don't want to *stay* on it. My plan is to go to the river, which will give us a break from Mother and Father—and give them a break from us. We'll visit with Roberto and, I hope, Miss LaBrix; get a firsthand, onboard look at the steamboat; then go home."

Ah, yes, Laurel thought. Catherine LaBrix, the beautiful, shy French girl Roberto had introduced to Jed.

Jed shook his head. "I probably don't have a chance."

"If she has brains as well as beauty, you do," Laurel said, and knew the minute it came out of her mouth that Jed would not pursue the subject. After a silence, he said, "When Father and I went rabbit hunting, we saw some things I want to show you. I'll tell you when we're getting close to them. In the meantime, Laur, keep your eyes on the road so you don't step into an earth tear, or trip on a weed or clod or something."

So he wanted to show her some things, and shield her from seeing other things.

A little later, Jed motioned to the left. "Father said those mounds are sand blows—sand the earthquakes blew up to the surface. But the quakes didn't just blow—they swallowed."

There, shaped like a funnel, was a pit wide enough at the top to set a small cabin in it. Laurel stopped walking. "How deep is it? Can we see it up close?"

Jed shook his head. "I took an up-close look, and my heart didn't stop pounding for five minutes. No telling where you'd land if you fell in that thing."

Laurel glanced around them. When she and Mother had gone to town with Father and Jed, they had gone in the wagon on this same road past these same woods

that now looked at one minute like a fairyland, and the next, a monster's lair. Vines and dead weeds were woven in a tapestry beside earthquake-created ponds so clear they reflected cloud puffs. But not far from the ponds, uprooted trees sprawled across winter-bare seedlings and layers of dried leaves.

"It gets worse as you go eastward," Jed said. "Along here, you need to be extra careful."

What, Laurel again wondered, did he not want her to see? Whatever it was, the sight could not be worse than the smell. She gasped, stopped walking, and grabbed his arm. Between the early morning dimness, the mangled road, and the soot-colored dirt, he apparently hadn't seen the snake. When he did, he said, "Black racer," at the same time Laurel realized it was a nonpoisonous snake.

"Father and I saw a couple of snakes when we went rabbit hunting," Jed told her. "They're sluggish, but I expect if you step on a sluggish water moccasin, he's as poisonous as a feisty one. So like I said, keep your eyes on the road."

A minute later, she looked off to her right, and knew what she smelled, and what he had not wanted her to see. A bog. An earthquake-created bog of vile-smelling, bubbling mud. Wild creatures caught in the ooze struggled to reach safety. The animals on dry ground, the watchers—deer and raccoons and an o'possum—were silent. Ordinarily, wild animals saw you

although you were not likely to see them, and disappeared into their domain, but these animals were beyond fearing humans. "Oh, Jed," she said, and the words were like a moan, "we have to do something."

"Do what?" he asked gruffly, and she knew he was right. They could do nothing; they were as helpless as the watchers.

They were soon in town, or, properly, the city. The City of New Madrid. It seemed unreal, as if she and Jed were walking inside a nightmare landscape. Every frame house had fallen; log houses looked unstable. The ground had sunk, and cracks ran in every direction. Two dogs chewed on a piece of raw meat; a gaunt yellow tomcat sat on an upside-down rain barrel. Sickening odors fouled the air. There were some tents, but she saw only one person, a humpbacked old woman, picking through the rubble.

Jed hurried on. "Roberto said around sixty boats are in the cove and tied up to willow bars in the bayou," he said close to her ear.

There it was: the cove. From the day he had first seen it, the cove had fascinated Jed. River men still called it *L'Anse à la Graisse*—the Cove of Grease—the name the French had given it when they owned this land and supplied so much bear and buffalo lard to traders en route to Natchez and New Orleans. She, too, had found the bustle fun—which made the scene before them even more nightmarish.

On the bank, men, women, and children, white and black and bronze, waited with their clothing bundles for the steamboat. Barges and flatboats scraped and bumped each other; their cargo added a bedlam of sound: cows bawling, pigs squealing, turkeys gobbling. The stink of rotting flesh and human and animal wastes filled her nostrils; great chunks of the bank had broken away and fallen into the river, which eddied and swirled, sucking in and spitting out trees, boards, logs, and animal carcasses.

Trembling, Laurel closed her eyes. She did not realize Roberto was there until he walked up and wrapped his strong arms around her, as if to protect her from the stench and sight and sound of death.

# CHAPTER 10

**R**oberto's man-smell stirred a sense-memory in Laurel of Father's comforting her when she was a child and had a nightmare. Cradling her in his arms, he had told her the darkness would give way to light, and she would see that the world was beautiful.

The world was not beautiful. It was ugly, and misery prevailed. In Roberto's arms, she sobbed. When the weeping subsided, he stepped back from her, shook hands with Jed, and motioned for them to come with him. As they walked, it became quieter. When they stopped, they could still see the cove, but here sound came as a murmur rather than a roar. Jed and Roberto could talk.

She would as soon not talk, at least for a while. Her nose was stopped up from crying, and next it would be dripping and she had forgotten to bring a . . . Wait. She remembered something. Mother had told her this morning that she had put a piece of material in her dress pocket to serve as a handkerchief square. When she took it from her pocket, she almost started crying again. Mother had torn off a piece of her own petticoat.

Laurel wiped her eyes and blew her nose and, as she put the square back in her pocket, turned her head to look behind her. Standing less than fifteen feet away, a beautiful dark-haired female—only a year or two older than she—gazed at them. Seconds later, Roberto and Jed turned their heads, and Laurel knew it was Roberto she silently beckoned.

"Roberto!" she said, as if she had just realized he was there, "Quel plaiser de vous voir!"

Laurel realized only vaguely that she had covered the split in her top lip with her fingers even as Roberto said, "It is a pleasure to see you, too, Catherine."

His voice did not hold warmth or happy surprise, and it occurred to Laurel that he was not really glad to see Catherine at all, but wanted Jed and her to know what she had said. Even while Roberto spoke, Catherine came toward them, her full blue-black skirt, beneath which Laurel thought there must be at least two petticoats, folding and unfolding.

When Catherine reached them, Roberto said to Laurel, "May I introduce Miss Catherine LaBrix? Miss LaBrix, Miss Laurel Mawston." To Catherine, he said, "You know Jed Mawston, I believe.

Laurel drew in her breath. Catherine LaBrix! The girl Jed had spoken about with such yearning.

At the same time that Laurel said, "How do you do," Catherine said, "Laurel, what a lovely name." She then looked at Jed, lowered her long, silky lashes, and murmured, "Bon matin, Jedidiah," as if she were shy—which female instinct told Laurel was skilled pretense.

Jed's face turned red, and the first time he tried to speak, his voice failed him. He cleared his throat, then said, "You look very pretty today, Miss LaBrix."

"Merci beaucoup," she murmured. After a few moments of awkward silence, she said, "It was a pleasure to meet you, Laurel. And to see you again, Jedidiah. I must speak with someone else going on the steamboat." In a cool voice, she said, "Au revoir, Roberto."

"Buenos dias," he said, and his voice was not cool; it was indifferent. Or perhaps he had feigned indifference. No, Laurel decided; he hadn't. In fact, she doubted that Roberto could pretend any more than Catherine LaBrix could refrain from pretending.

Jed's eyes followed Catherine; he made his decision and hastened to catch up with her. Roberto, Laurel thought, had no choice. Being a gentleman, he had to stay with her.

The din assailed her nerves, the cold dampness burrowed deeper into her bones, and every time more of the bank slid into the river, she flinched. Surely the steamboat would soon be here. Maybe she and Jed could go home now and tell Mother and Father that it had not stopped, which would be no bigger lie than saying they had gone aboard but had given up their space to . . . She would have to invent two dear people whose names they did not learn. Since at least a hundred people with baggage and hopeful faces were waiting for the *New Orleans* to arrive, that would be easy enough.

A shout rose above the noise from the cove and the river's throb. "It's coming! The steamboat's coming!"

The *New Orleans* was well out in the channel, and if she had not already known, Laurel thought, she did now. No matter how much he needed supplies, or how much compassion he had, with dead animals and debris floating around, Captain Roosevelt would not attempt to bring the steamboat in here. To do so would be to place Mrs. Roosevelt, their children, and the crew in even greater jeopardy. He had no recourse but to proceed and stop for wood and other supplies at a more suitable place.

She turned her head to look at Roberto. His face was sad. He had worked on a keelboat; he had surely doubted Captain Roosevelt would stop at New Madrid no matter how much he needed supplies. He should

have told these people! He should have told his mes-
senger to tell Father he had doubts.

The anger went as swiftly as it had come. Would Father, or these frightened, waiting people have listened?
What if Roberto had said Captain Roosevelt would not
stop and people had gone home—and Captain Roosevelt had stopped after all? Hot tears came, and she
did not know why. She swiped at the tears, closed her
eyes, and covered her mouth.

Roberto took her hand, moved it away from her
mouth, and gently, sweetly kissed her as the *New Orleans* passed New Madrid and continued its downriver
journey.

## CHAPTER 11

*W*alking the earthquake-fractured road toward home, Laurel did not look to either side of it; nor did she make any effort to talk with Jed, who was immersed in his own thoughts. Roberto had kissed her! Kissed her full on her lips. And when he lifted his head, there had been no hint of revulsion on his face.

As they neared home, she tucked away the memory and envisioned Mother weeping and Father's eyes filling with tears when she and Jed walked into the yard. She had not considered Ranger's superior senses of hearing and smell. He trotted up the road to meet them. Father came to the front of the house, turned his head, and called, "Mother!" Mother joined him,

and they came to greet Jed and her.

Mother, whose eyes were already red from weeping, cried with Laurel while Father and Jed cleared their throats and shifted from one foot to the other. As they all went toward the backyard, Laurel and Jed told about the destruction in New Madrid, the townspeople living in tents, and the people weeping when the *New Orleans* passed New Madrid by.

They told about seeing Roberto, and Laurel started to tell about Catherine, the beautiful French girl, but decided not to lest she upset Jed.

That afternoon, after she and Jed had taken a long nap, they all huddled near the fire. Laurel said, "Father, between the springhouse boards, and branches from the woods, could we build a kind of lean-to? It wouldn't actually lean against the house; it would just be higher at one end. Tall support sticks at one end, and short ones at the other."

Father frowned and, Laurel thought, started to shake his head, but he didn't. "It's worth a try. And we have enough bearskins to make a warm carpet."

When they had finished, Mother said, "It's beautiful!"

"I don't think I'd go that far," Father said. He looked at the lot and the collapsed barn. "Let us now make an animal shelter."

They were exhausted but proud by the time they finished that project. Not one of the animals, not even

the supposedly intelligent brood sow, would have aught to do with it.

Three days later, on Sunday, December twenty-second, they went to services in the churchyard. On the few previous occasions when all four of them had gone into town and left him, it had not upset Ranger. This time it did, even though Father told him they depended on him to keep guard while they were gone.

The *New Orleans* was still a big topic of conversation among the congregation, and Mr. Williams told about something that had happened before it reached New Madrid. Shortly before the *New Orleans*—which the Chickasaw Indians called *Penelore,* "fire canoe"— left the Ohio River, the Chickasaws had given chase. In many canoes, they had come almost even with the steamboat.

The men on the *New Orleans* fed wood as fast as possible; it had gotten up enough steam, and therefore speed, to pull ahead of all save one great, long canoe, which kept apace until the Chickasaws tired. "That steamboat proved its worth, right there," Mr. Williams said. "It's a good thing, too, else those Injuns would have boarded it and killed everybody aboard."

"Bosh!" Father said. "The Chickasaws love a contest."

In the silence, Laurel could hear a far-off crow call; then Father, realizing how gravely he had upset Mr.

Williams, chuckled and said, "It's a good story, though."

A few minutes later, Reverend Stewart greeted the small congregation, then led them in prayer. While they stood in the yard, shivering beneath a leaden sky, he read the account of Jesus' birth given by Luke, the apostle and physician, and spoke briefly about the hope Jesus' coming had brought for mankind.

When they sang in closing "The First Noel," and came to the end of the first verse—*on a cold winter's night that was so deep*—Laurel thought that it could not have been any colder than it was here. Mrs. Jensen, who led the singing, went into the second verse.

The moment they finished it, Reverend Stewart said, "Amen!" before Mrs. Jensen could go to verse three.

When they were out of the churchyard, Jed said, "Considering that between earthquakes and Christmas there haven't been that many people at a service since we moved here, it must have been awful hard on Reverend Stewart to give such a short sermon. But it's easy to figure out why he did. When he said that last 'Amen,' he was shaking like a leaf."

"Jedidiah!" Mother said.

But Father, Laurel realized, was turning red in the face. When he could control it no longer, his laughter burst forth and, her mouth twitching, Mother said, "You are as bad as your son!" She then said to Father,

"Since we're this close, I suppose we should call on Mrs. Greene."

Mrs. Greene, a woman in her mid-forties who smoked a cob pipe, was the congregation's despair. Her three children had died of milk sickness soon after Laurel's family moved to New Madrid County. Then Mr. Greene's mule kicked him in the head, and he died. Mrs. Greene had stopped coming to church and had taken up the pipe-smoking.

"Very well," Father said. "We will go to see Mrs. Greene. But if I cannot go into my own house, I will certainly not go into hers."

Laurel's thoughts went to the cove, and to Roberto. She had probably only imagined that his heart, like hers, had quickened when he embraced and kissed her.

"I agree," Mother told Father. "We will call to her, and if she opens the door, wish her a merry Christmas."

As Mother and Father went on to see Mrs. Greene, Laurel shook her head to dismiss Roberto from her thoughts. An opportunity was at hand.

When she and Jed arrived back at their own house, she stood looking at it. She pictured the dried red peppers hanging by the fireplace. Mother particularly missed having them to season rabbit and squirrel stews. She pictured her writing tablet and the ink bottle. The events of this December were like none they had

experienced before or would again. And she could not record them.

"You look tired," she said to Jed.

"Aren't you?" he asked. "Isn't everybody?"

She sighed and nodded.

Giving each other the privacy they had always extended, they removed their church clothes and put on everyday garments—except Laurel didn't put on her shoes. "Why don't you stretch out a few minutes?" she asked Jed.

He yawned. "I think I will. After all, even if I had anything to do, I couldn't. When I was little, I dreaded Sundays. At least we no longer have to wear our best bib and tucker the whole day through."

The minute Jed began sleep-breathing—and as Mother said, he obviously had a clear conscience because otherwise he could not go to sleep so quickly—Laurel peeled off her stockings, slipped out of the lean-to, went to the front door, and slowly pushed it open.

She could not do it. If she were injured or killed, Father would forever afterward think he had not been forceful enough, and would blame himself.

## CHAPTER 12

*W*e called from the yard, and Mrs. Greene opened the door—and invited us to come in," Mother told Laurel and Jed when she and Father came home.

"I warned her that by continuing to live in her house, she was tempting fate," Father said.

Mother, looking at the Mawstons' leaning house, nodded. "To which she replied that she reckoned she would go right on tempting the old buzzard."

"I'll do it," Father told Mother.

Mother shook her head. "No, dear, you are larger than I, and if I may say so, not as light afoot." She removed her shoes and stockings, went inside, and brought out the breadboard and mixing bowl. Inside

72

the bowl, she had put the string of dried red peppers, the ink, and Laurel's writing tablet and quill. "I do not think I—or anyone—should go back into our house," Mother said. "It groaned and muttered."

On Tuesday, December twenty-fourth, two days after Mother went into the house, Laurel wrote in her journal:

*It is Christmas Eve in the year of our Lord, 1811, and the most wonderful thing happened today! More than a hundred people—the entire population of Little Prairie, which the earthquakes demolished—arrived, on horseback and afoot, in New Madrid. We are going into town to greet them.*

Jed, who went often to see Catherine LaBrix, had told them that a few boats were cautiously moving in and out of the cove, and that boatmen said the earthquakes had ravaged towns and woods and farmlands far up and down the river. The boatmen had not known, though, about the people coming from Little Prairie, who had not walked close to the bank for fear it would crumble. No one knew about them until they were in view.

Picturing New Madrid as a safe haven, and knowing that their cattle would "remember" the long-ago days when their forebears were wild and fend for

themselves, the people had left most of them and set out with their dogs and cats and horses. They had not realized that they would have to cross rises and streams and get through deep woods. Nor had they taken into account that while New Madrid was only about thirty miles upriver as the crow flies, the walking distance would be greater.

Bitter cold had swept down on them, but the ice on streams flowing into the river was not thick enough to support their horses. Two had broken through the ice, and in panic from cold and fear, drowned.

New Madridians had welcomed the travelers, Jed told them, and Father and Mother decided the Mawstons should go into town to greet them. Soon after they reached the town, Jed excused himself, and Laurel knew he had gone in search of Catherine.

The Little Prairie folk, Laurel thought, were remarkable. Though all were weary, and some were ill, they joked and laughed and were obviously pleased that they were so welcomed.

Before they returned home, Father said, he would like to go down to the cove. There, where boats screeched and animals bawled just as they had the day the steamboat had passed, conditions had worsened. Laurel looked around for Roberto. If she saw him, she told herself, she would lift her chin and give him a cool glance. Instead, when she saw him coming, she wanted to wrap her arms around him. He was gaunt,

and deep hollows lay beneath his eyes. He and Mother and Father greeted each other. He then turned to Laurel and said, "Miss Mawston." He reached out his hand as if to touch her face, but a man's strident voice shouted from the cove, "Señor Vega, we need help down here!" and he turned and walked away.

A few days after Christmas, the Mawstons had two special visitors. Smoke came and brought with her a huge, wary tom that had not only the same coloring but the same markings as his wild relative, the tiger. Mother made a gesture of friendship, and he spat at her. "You have made your sentiments abundantly clear," Mother said, and Father said, "If Smoke hadn't obviously chosen that fellow, I'd stretch his hide."

When they retired for the night, Smoke and her mate were still there. But they were gone the next morning. Mother sighed and said, "We will not see her again."

During the following days, Laurel's concern for Jed increased. Despite the cold, he made trips into town. For the first time ever, he did not confide in her, and one night she heard him crying.

## CHAPTER 13

*S*mall earthquakes continued to regularly jolt them, but Laurel's stomach-hollowing fear each time one hit lessened. It also helped that a warm spell came toward the middle of January. Jed, who still went often into town, said the ice in the cove had broken up. Around nine o'clock on Thursday morning, January twenty-third, Mother and Laurel were hanging the bedding on the clothesline to air when the sulfur smell became stronger. The ground began to ripple. They immediately lay down on their sides; by the time they pulled up their knees and curled themselves into a ball shape, the ripple had become a swaying.

Through the noise of trees cracking and falling, and

birds and animals screaming, Laurel heard Jed shouting and yelling at God. When the swaying stopped enough for her to get to her hands and knees and in position to see through the ground dust and haze, Father was crawling toward him. Father pulled Jed into his arms as if he were a little boy, and Laurel's pain for him gave way to fury. She would tear out Catherine LaBrix's hair!

During the days following the earthquake, a sense of despair hung like a dark, heavy curtain that not even Mother could find strength to push aside.

Roberto came, riding the same mule his servant Tomas had ridden when he came to tell them when the *New Orleans* would reach New Madrid. He had come to see how they fared, Roberto said, and to ask if he might walk a way with Miss Mawston.

Laurel glared at him. She had not seen him since Christmas Eve, when the people from Little Prairie arrived, and he had been too preoccupied to do more than greet her. No, that was not right. She was being unfair. He had reached out to touch her, but someone had called for his help. Very well, but he could have at least chosen to come when she had bathed and dressed as well as possible. Instead, she was unkempt and surely smelling of fear-sweat and smoke.

"If my daughter wishes to walk with you, Mr. Vega," Father said, "she has my permission."

She did not *wish* to walk with him! She did not

wish to be with him at all!

They had gone only a short way up the ruptured road when Roberto said, "Will you marry me?"

She whirled to face him. "You mock me!" she said fiercely. "Is it not enough that I am weary and my hair and skin are dirty and I have a—a harelip?! Why are you doing this?" She would not cry. She had done that, cried in his arms like a child when the smell of death at the cove had overwhelmed her.

"Why do I want to marry you?" he said. "Hmm. Considering your wicked temper, that is a good question."

"My wicked temper! I will have you know, sir, that I am ordinarily even-tempered and, and shy."

He laughed and pulled her to his chest. She could feel his heartbeat and hear a screech owl's soft, quavering call.

"When the world is right again," he said, "and it will be, my love—will you marry me?"

"Yes," she said, but after a moment, she looked up at him and asked, "Why must we wait until the world is right again?"

His laughter startled some crows in a big persimmon tree; they scolded and flew away with a rush of wings.

 CHAPTER 14

*T*he tremors had become mild, with longer spaces between them, when another earthquake, worse than any so far, stuck at three in the morning on February seventh. The house collapsed, burying everything still inside, but that was of small consequence. Galahad went berserk, ran as if he had gone crazy, fell, and broke his right foreleg. After he shot Galahad, Mother wrapped her arms around Father and did not try to hush his hoarse sobbing.

In midmorning, Reverend Stewart, his eyes red from lack of sleep, and darting from one point to another as if he expected at any moment to be attacked, came. He told them that the river had thrown up gigantic

waves, that banks had caved in, and land near the river had dropped lower and lower.

"The townspeople?" Father asked, and Laurel's heart seemed to pause while she awaited Reverend Stewart's answer.

"They have moved their tents farther and farther back. The banks are caving in, you see. The land has dropped lower and lower. You must leave; we must all leave."

He told them then that the river had thrown a great crashing, roaring, thundering wave onto the west bank. When the wave went back into the channel, it took with it animals, boats, houses, and a whole grove of cottonwood trees. It drove flatboats, barges, and keelboats up St. John's Bayou. It threw other huge boats onto dry land, then jerked them back into the river. On land, quicksand and mud bogs buried struggling animals. Falling trees killed many others but only broke the bones of some, so that they screamed in agony until death came. A man fell into one of the funnel-shaped sand blows with water pooled in its bottom and drowned.

Reverend Stewart's voice, a voice that had still been strong and forceful as late as a week ago, trembled as he told how the river had parted crosswise, running upstream on one side of the part and downstream on the other. Boats slammed to the waterless road across the riverbed and landed upright on the coarse sand.

Men jumped out of the boats and ran to safety before the walls of water closed and silenced the screams of caged animals and fowls.

"Yes," Father said, "we must all leave. We still have coffee. Will you not share a cup with us, Reverend Stewart?"

"I have not time," their minister said. "I must spread the word. We must all leave." He left, saying the same words again.

That evening, Laurel wrote in her journal:

> *How small we humans are. How little we know. Five weeks ago, on the evening of December 15, I wrote that this move would be our last, because New Madrid would become a great city. Father and Mother say our poor pastor is right, and I, too, know New Madrid is doomed, and we must all leave.*

All but a few people who lived in or near New Madrid decided to leave. They agreed to meet at Tywappity Hill, a small settlement about forty miles northwest of what had been the city of New Madrid.

The Mawstons still had their wagon; the mules, Samson and Pretty Girl; and a few frail, demented chickens. They put the chickens in a coop and placed the coop in the wagon. Father hitched Samson and Pretty Girl to the wagon; Jed tied Dolly to a rope

fastened to the tailgate.   Ranger, nervously panting much of the time, looking and acting many years older than he had a year ago, walked beside the wagon.

Laurel and Roberto were married at Tywappity Hill, where Jed and Rachel's friendship began.   Jed and Rachel were married in St. Louis, where many of the New Madrid people eventually settled.

## AFTERWORD

On the east side of the river, a little south of New Madrid, the February seventh earthquake drowned all the Chickasaw people who lived there and formed Reelfoot Lake, a shallow lake fourteen miles long and four and a half miles wide, in Tennessee. It was named for the Chickasaw chief Reelfoot, whose clubfoot caused him to "reel" when he walked. Big Lake in Arkansas is also an earthquake lake, and both are sanctuaries for a variety of fish and birds, as are smaller earthquake-created lakes and bayous.

New Madrid bloomed again; few towns can rival its beauty. From an observation platform, you can look at the wide, rippling Mississippi River; at the museum,

you can see relics of long-ago times and watch the seismograph record small earth movements you do not feel.

A small earthquake—magnitude 4.6 on the scale devised in 1935 by Charles Richter—shook New Madrid on May 3, 1991, and was felt in six states. In 1999, at the conclusion of a study of the New Madrid Fault, Karl Mueller, a geologist at the University of Colorado in Boulder, wrote that the panel estimated the 1811-1812 earthquakes reached a magnitude of 7.5. They affected more than a million square miles and, despite the sparse population, killed at least two thousand people.